Ulterior Magics

Poems on Magic, the Universe, and Everything Else

by Nathan Lathroum

Table of Contents

Author's Foreword

This collection of poems, which I've titled "Ulterior Magics", serves as the capstone of a required class in my college education. The class itself is referred to as "Self, Society, and Cosmos"; regardless of a student's discipline, all are required to take it, though stories of the class range from studies of magic's history to understanding ancient battle tactics. The class I ended up with was entirely on the magical side of that spectrum. We studied all sorts of ancient magic, from Ancient Egypt and Mesopotamia to India and Rome; even prehistoric Europe made an appearance. Though we only had a single semester to delve into these topics, the pacing of the class allowed for brief yet informative studies of each major derivative. Instead of a typical final assessment, our professor opted to assign a final project instead. Having prior experience as more than several kinds of writers, I decided to write a series of poems to demonstrate my understanding and perspective on the class. And instead of a small collection for an easy grade, I decided I wanted to go above and beyond (surprise, surprise): not only was I going to write a series of poems on magic, I was going to write out an entire book of poetry on the subject.

As previously mentioned, the title of the book is “Ulterior Magics”. This is partially due to the similarity to ‘ulterior motives’, giving the title a particularly nice ring, but it’s also due to the definition of ‘ulterior’. If you were unaware, ‘ulterior’ means secret or hidden, much like the word ‘occult’; the two are quite similar. Though, to be honest, most of the title’s creation is because of its similarity to ‘ulterior motives’. I’m a sucker for rhymes and phrases.

Part of the final project assignment for the class includes answering a brief series of questions related to the coursework. The questions are as follows: How do you see yourself in the cosmos? Can we still find the presence of magic, religion, and science in western society? And finally, have your ideas on magic changed since the beginning of the course? To save some material for later, I will address all of these questions (as well as any other remaining loose ends) in the closing of this book. First, I will present the series of poems I have written and compiled here.

Each section contains poems I felt fit its category, with some categories being intentionally vague while others seem quite specific. The same goes for the poems themselves: some are intentionally vague, and some will leave little room for the imagination. This is by design. All the decisions here are not without their own set of intentions.

Every poem is, of course, up for the reader's own interpretation. I can explain the reasoning behind each poem, but only to an extent. Aside from the reader deciding whether or not to believe my reasoning, each poem may mean something completely different when discussed between two readers. That is, again, by design. To reiterate, all the decisions made here are not without their own set of intentions.

"Ulterior Magics" will be the third complete book I have written. My first novel, "King Between Worlds", is a magical fantasy novel. Its sequel, "Queen of the Seas", takes place with direct correlation to its predecessor. Many incomplete story outlines and brainstorming notes lie in between "Queen of the Seas" and "Ulterior Magics"; perhaps that is again by design. Perhaps not. Either way, it seems fitting that my next published writing still connects back to my previous works.

And with that, dear reader, I send you off to explore these poems for yourself.

Do not take everything I say for fact, of course; interpret the words how you feel they should be interpreted. Understand them the way you feel they should be understood. And, above all, make all your decisions with your own set of intentions.

Rock on!

Sincerely,
Nathan Lathroum

I. UNIVERSAL TRUTHS

* * * * * * * * * * * * * * * * * * * *

"The Purpose of Life"

Ages past and times before,
Bearing what the people bore.
Broken bones and fossils hence
Serve to show their recompense.

Here we look and here we see
An ancient form of you and me.
A living man since lived ago
In times so different than we know.

Beside him sit what surely be
His closest friends and family.
Look, see here, thc spot I point.
Behind the leg, right at the joint.

It's clear to see it cracked right here,
Visible when we aren't near.
With such a break at such a time,
It should have made this man to die.

But look! His bones are far too old.

He made it past what we foretold.
Ancient? Granted, no, not quite,
But far from youthful candlelight.

He should have perished at the break,
For death was meant to overtake.
But look! Right there, the spot I point.
You see his healing at the joint.

The implications are immense.
It serves to show their recompense.
And look! Right here, at which I point.
We see the healing on his joint.

"Mundane Magics"

The waking businessman will say
He must be working every day.
His wrinkled face is on display,
His youthful dreams are sent away.

But look! There's more to life than this.
There's more than discontent to bliss.

Many magics seem of times
And worlds so far away,
But even magics can be found
In everyday mundane.

And hear! There still is more than this.
There's more than magics turned to bliss.

Just look beneath you at your feet,
The dandelion through concrete.
Just look above you in the sky,
A pair of doves come soaring by.

So feel! There's magic to be found.
No matter sides, it's all around.

The greatest magics, so they say,
Are found in the mundane.

"The Call of the Bard"

Whenever magic comes to mind,
The mind doth wander in the sky.
Yet even further into thought,
A melody itself is brought.

For magics of all kinds are found
In every form, in every town.
Just listen close and hear the call,
And match the music down the hall.

It starts with taps,
The ink of pen.
A little dance,
The hum of men.

A hop, a skip,
A step to be.
A real musician's
Memory.

A jump, a skip,
A dance, a spin.

A tune,
A song,
A win.

"Impermanence"

Some flowers come back every year,
While others seem to disappear.
I tell you as the winters near
That's not what makes it last.

Some magics work behind the scenes
While wizards work and waters gleam.
I tell you as they sow the seams
That's not what makes it last.

From ages old and long ago,
The human mind has longed to know.
Some may try where others go.
That's not what makes it last.

A shining stem upon the grass
Attracts the eyes with every pass.
Although the rose with beauty holds,
That's not what makes it last.

The fishes swim inside the stream
As boiling kettles rise with steam.
And though the taste of tea is dream,
That's not what makes it last.

What people seek is yet within,

Their smile on their sun-lit chin.
It’s not yet too late to begin.
That’s what makes it last.

"On Elder Teachings"

Oftentimes we're given words
We do not understand.
We leap to our conclusions
Based on separate circumstance.

And though we try and fail to see
The meaning of the scribe,
The wonder lies within the words
That we have cast aside.

Oftentimes we're meant to learn
From lessons of the old.
We're given tasks and guidance from
The stories we are told.

And though we try and fail to see
The meaning of the words,
We ought to sit and settle down
And listen to the birds.

II. REASONS FOR PLAGUES

* *

"Housewifely Secrets"

In days of yore and times of old,
Such secrets housewives did behold.
And in their sly and secret ways
Handled every work of days.

Told by many of their place
Among the gallant human race.
Books were written, stories told,
Of living ways alike the old.

Kept away from spoken speech
And granted only minor feats.
Such was the way it had since been,
And would, was thought, always begin.

Yet now we understand the past
More so than lifetimes prior last.
The secrets kept in homes and towns
Were much less smiles, more so frowns.

With all the secrets told by men
Of all what would begin again,
Tradition kept its steady pace

Until the secrets found their place.

Some were written nicely.
Some were called housewifely.

"On Revoking Authority"

Reference yet again is made
To times long since forgotten.
Calling back again is done
To times of foreign cotton.

Many times did this take place
Among those many years.
And many times did this erupt
From foreign people's fears.

Begone! they shouted at the man
Who they had not yet known.
Begone! they said to him again,
For you're not what we've sown.

He didn't speak their languages
And couldn't read their text,
But they had pressed upon him
Categories quite immense.

With words attached that rang no bells,
Except to foreign ears,
The man was left to live his life
While looked down by his peers.

"Bewitchment of Endor"

There once was told a story
In a holiest of text:
It followed dear King Saul
And his crusade against the hex.

He drove the witches from his land
And burned them at the stake.
He chased the wizards far away
And sought their lives to take.

Yet even after battles fought,
His future was uncertain.
He drove the magic from his land,
He felt he closed the curtain.

His prayers had gone unanswered
For too many days a time.
He felt the sting of deep regret
And left to grasslands climb.

If nothing else, his trip was fueled
By fear of the unknown.
He wanted God to tell him all
That ever would be known.

Alas, what King Saul failed to grasp

Was that he wasn't true.
His journey outward certainly
Was not what he's to do.

After what had been some time
Of journeying afoot,
He found the place his sights were set,
In where his trust was put.

The wooden shack lay still and silent
Deep among the trees.
King Saul approached it further in
And walked so cautiously.

Inside? A woman called a witch
By those who would desert her.
King Saul had entered in the home
And promised not to hurt her.

She took his word and, by request,
Was made to summon Samuel.
But much to King Saul's great remorse,
He criticized his rule.

And furthermore, Samuel had said
King Saul was running thin.
His enemy would battle him,
His enemy would win.

And as foretold, the followed morn,
King Saul was swift defeated.
At least before he left the hut,
The Witch made sure he ate.

“Common Strikes”

It seems quite common, looking back,
That common strikes the learn-ed.
But if one gives it moment’s thought,
They’ll find ideals deserted.

For often times the compromise
Of living altogether
Is brought with wealthier disgrace
That nary makes it better.

And looking further, one may find
A new and shocking truth:
That learn-ed often strike down first
Upon the common’s roof.

"On Magical Wars"

Drive the magic far away
To never be forgiven.
All those who will try to stay,
Farther away are driven.

Look! The war! It wrecks the land,
Dripping blood from royal hand.

Drive the living far away
To never be forgiven.
All those who will start to pray,
Farther away are driven.

Look! The war! It splits the land.
Hear the ring of the evil band.

III. RIGHTS OF MAGIC

* * * * * * * * * * * * * * * * * * *

"The Last Great Magician"

A man who mastered science!
That's what all the people said.
But they had lacked the knowledge
Of the thoughts inside his head.

Our first and greatest scientist!
They boasted to the crowd.
But they had lacked the knowledge
Of what he had since allowed.

For back alone in cellars deep
And attics up on high,
The scientist was noting steps
Of alchemical kind.

Yet all his notes were left to turn
To ashes and to dust,
Found only by an accident
Before they turned to rust.

It seemed that even in his time,
His works were quite unknown.
He worked and toiled and slaved away

In secret rooms at home.

A man who mastered science!
Oh, only if they knew
That the man who mastered science
Was a good magician, too.

“As Above, So Below”

A tablet bright and green
Gave wisdom to the world
In forms and tales and phrases
Its languages unfurled.

And one so often quoted
By the few and many:
As above, so below;
It means as much as any.

But where’s the tale?
You speak aloud.
Where is the magic art?

Look deeper inward, student child,
And find it in the heart.

"The Meaning of Abracadabra"

Broken down those years ago
And used to mend a sickness,
The strength and power of the word
Relied on spoken quickness.

Beginning full, and thusly turning
Smaller until gone,
The sickness then was overturned
Like queen unto a pawn.

Behold! Here now I saw to you
The power of the word.
Remember, when you lie in bed,
The meaning you have heard.

Abracadabra
Abracadabr
Abracadab
Abracada
Abracad
Abraca
Abrac
Abra
Abr
Ab
A
It is gone.

“The Three Separations”

Transactional, how brilliant!
Transformational, what grace!
Transcendent, how it’s marvelous!
I see it on your face.

The first is one that, in its works,
Demands a thing to trade.
Your time, an herb, a food of sorts
Could all turn offer made.

The second one is less a deal
Than it is so an act.
To take one thing and make it else
Is what it doth attract.

The third and final one is such
That deals with inner self;
To elevate a higher place
Upon the cosmic shelf.

I see it on your face, I know
The look of deeper thought.
Continue thinking, questioning,
And try the one you ought.

IV. ALCHEMICAL BEGINNINGS

* *

"Chasing the Green Lion"

Upon a wide plateau stood a fortress,
Its coffers ever deep.
It housed the wisest men of the land
Where secrets hid in sleep.

Ruling ever mightily over the fortress
Was a Fearsome King.
He awoke one morn to find he heard
The battle bell ring.

Upon entering his war chamber,
Told by magicians three:
A green lion stood idle on the land
Adjacent to thee.

The Fearsome King called forth his men,
Readying to march.
They left at once through the formidable
Fortress's grand arch.

He waved his sword through the air,
Calling them to fight.
After this, he witnessed death
Of every noble knight.

Why? he called out to the beast,
Giving no response.
Why my people? he cried,
And the lion left at once.

The King went home defeated,
Remembering forever since.
As such, he dubbed his loyal servants
Alchemists.

"Growing the Tree of Diana"

After the hunt,
Before the stone,
There lies the Tree of Diana.

Made of crystal,
Made with care,
It blooms with the lantana.

The silver tree,
The stepping stone,
The magic clearly shows.

It thrusts its branches,
Draws its lines,
And grows from the unknown.

Saturn's Tree, the sister tree,
Calls out in tune with her.
Together singing, twisting roots
In efforts to confer.

In metals lost and substance found,
We seek to seek the pure.
With flame in hand and heart in mind,
We follow it with her.

"With Intent to Transform"

Transformation is no stranger
To the working world of men.
Transformation is no danger
To the ink within the pen.

Transformation is no accident
When purposely concurred.
Transformation is intent
With every spoken word.

Transforming one to make anew
A different kind of thing.
Transforming sun to make the moon
Displayed on every ring.

Transforming all to make again
A different sort of type.
Transforming fall to make again
The followed winter's gripe.

Having long since been transformed,
The sunshine sings of youth.
What it has been has since been lost
Within pursuit of truth.

Having long since been transformed,

The shining light is found.
It springs itself upon the maker,
Making him profound.

"The Story of Chema"

This is the story of Chema,
The princess of a far land.
She thought highly of her parents
And their twofold ruling hand.

Alas, one day she soon was met
With ever such a plight:
The sleeping quarters had been raided
Sometime in the night.

With neither of her parents left,
She took upon the queenship.
And so was the story of Chema,
Who had melted into kinship.

V. LANGUAGE OF THE STARS

* *

"On Charting One's Birth"

Upon the birth of a child,
An astrologist would arrive.
Some would call them early on
So they appeared on time.

The more accurate the time of birth,
The better charted map,
For even days or hours off
Could register mishap.

In times of old and centuries
That have yet to recall,
The charting of a person's birth
Had carried wherewithal.

Even kings of foreign lands,
And queens of those still near,
Would call upon astrologists
To calm their cosmic fear.

And even in our current age
As we look back to then,
Astrologists are still called forth
To tell us where and when.

"On Charting One's Life"

When it was seen as necessary
Charting someone's birth,
A just-as-vital step to this
Was periodic worth.

Every many days or so,
Astrologists would tell
To help with finding signs of sick
And where their fortunes fell.

And it was categorically
Managed and believed
That finding risings of the planets
Chang-ed what they see.

For one knew not ahead of time
What illness fell to thee;
The ministers of medicine
Fell secondly to we.

And yet! the sickness of the heart
And sickness of the mind
Was found to be the stars' alignment
Many different times.

To cure one's shaking fever, say,

A crush-ed skull of man
To since be drunken through a mix
Of water from the land.

Every many days or so,
Astrologists would tell
To help with finding signs of sick
And where their fortunes fell.

"On Charting One's World"

When it was seen as necessary
Charting someone's birth,
A just-as-vital step to this
Was periodic worth.

And in such steps a man could take,
And what he could have done,
Astrologists would chart the skies
And study on the sun.

They plotted movements of the stars
On maps and charts and graphs.
They found the motions of the moon
And kept it squared in halves.

The dances of the constellations
Beckoning with call
Had drawn attention from the men
Who sought to study all.

And if the question had arisen
If it were for naught,
They'd simply point to moon and tide
And ask if they mistaught.

VI. TRAVELING MAGICS

* *

"The Emerald Tablet"

Authored by he who does not exist,
The Emerald Tablet in history sits.
It dictates the writings of he who was said,
Telling of his words as dead.

What does it say?
What does it mean?
Its mysteries waver,
In daylight they gleam.

Moving through ages and continents since,
The Emerald Tablet in history sits.
It tells of the knowledge one would seek,
Its words much describing what magic fits.

What does it say?
What does it mean?
Its mysteries waver,
In moonlight they gleam.

Still yet occult in each sense of the word,
The Emerald Tablet's soft echoes are
heard.

It tells of great workings of he who is false,
Found still in the arms of a corpse on a throne.

What does it say?
What does it mean?
Its mysteries waver,
In limelight they gleam.

“From Indian Spices”

Communication distantly
Had lent itself to error;
Rising costs of living spaces
Lent themselves to terror.

Imports from a foreign land
Were at first used in dishes,
Though later they were thought to be
Products of magic wishes.

All for the love of pepper!
All stemmed from the love of pepper!

After deep association
Into secret arts,
The Roman law had since forbid
The presence of its charts.

It started with a love of pepper!
It stemmed from a love of pepper!

Outlawed for use in magic,
Though only used in food,
Those who took part in the use of it
Were put in a magic brood.

It started with loving pepper!
It stemmed from loving pepper!

“On Discarded Amulets”

On the nature of discarded amulets,
There’s something to be learned.
If you look close and see the lines,
There’s wisdom to be earned.

Trace the bronze inscriptions
Made to counter curses

Hidden deep within the lines
And told within the verses

On the nature of discarded amulets
Displayed within museums,
Living relics of the past,
Lost in time’s mausoleums

Trace the copper lining
Forged to ensure

Hidden deep within the lines
Is magic to endure

On the nature of discarded amulets,
There’s wisdom to be earned.
Pay close attention to the words
Of ancients having yearned.

"Payment to the Oracle"

There once was a man on the mountaintop
Who lived in a wooden house.
He kept to himself and lived all alone,
As quiet as a mouse.

One day he wondered what his life
Was fated to become

What better way to document
What will and won't be done?

He traveled down to Valley Town
To meet up with someone

The man who was from the mountaintop
Stepped into an ancient home.
Inside there was an oracle
Who knew all that was known.

He asked the oracle what his life
Was fated to become

What better way to communicate
What will and won't be done?

He traveled down to Valley Town

To meet this very one

The oracle predicted fortune
Coming to his world.
Soon his life would prosper;
His good fortune has unfurled!

The oracle outstretched his hand
He pointed to it twice

He was a friendly fellow
But he wasn't very nice

"Ancestors of Time"

People we have known before
But since have lost to time
Are never truly lost;
In fact, they're only in their prime

Ancestors living with those who
Upon this Earth remain
May frequently support those who
Try goodness to obtain.

Occasionally offerings
Would be put into place.
Alters, tables, plates of food
Presented to a face.

Ancient paintings, distant lands,
Spiritual planes.
Old descendants, elder folks,
And living, waking strains.

Speaking with the ancestors,
Hello! You understand.
You've been through all of this before
And live in mystic lands.

Speaking with the ancestors,

Hello! We finally meet.
We talk about the present day
And all our present feats.

"The Water Town"

The river floods with water
And it damages the town.
Disdain emerges from the rubble,
Gathering around.

But yet! Was it not from the sea
That food and fish were caught?
And yet! Was it not from the sea
That livelihood was brought?

Cast further doubt not deep into
The waters of the ocean;
Take the fear unto one's self
As solitary token.

And yet! They build their walls of sea
To stop the flowing water.
And yet! They mold and shape the Earth
And think that they have got her.

The river floods with water
And it damages the town.
Disdain emerges from the rubble,
Gathering around.

Spread the fishes! Spread the housing

All across the sea!
Understand the river mean-eth
No ill will to thee.

"The First Unicorn"

Look! He shows
The unicorn's nose.

Look and adorn
The unicorn's horn.

Quick! Come hither,
And see for yourself,

The wizard transformed
A goat into else.

VII. ALCHEMICAL ENDINGS

* *

"The Blackening"

Based on European Folklore

The blackening, the blackening!
Make haste across the sky.
The toad leaps over water
And the raven sails the sky.

The blackening, the blackening!
Make haste across the land.
The toad runs after water
And the raven breaks the band.

The blackening, the blackening!
Make haste across the hills.
The toad runs under branches
And the raven sicks its wills.

The blackening, the blackening!
Make haste across the river.
The toad is getting hungry
And the raven longs for dinner.

The blackening, the blackening!
Make haste across the sea.

The toad is jumping faster
And the raven hunts for thee.

The blackening, the blackening!
Make haste across the road.
The toad runs through the valley
And the raven eats the toad.

"The Whitening"

Based on European Folklore

A white swan floats on water tops
Upon the quiet sea.
It settles by a skeleton
That might as well be thee.

Though nary conversation
Could be offered from the bones,
The swan had sought its shelter
As a temporary home.

The lightning cracked the hills below,
The thunder cracked the sky.
The swan had fallen fast asleep
Beneath its watchful eye.

"The Reddening"

Based on European Folklore

Look in the sky! A pelican
Is soaring through the air.
It keeps its eyes on lands below
And sees the nesting there.

It sails the breeze and settles in
Beneath a broken tree.
A gathering of baby birds:
Chee, chee, chee!

The pelican, in charge of them,
Outstretches of its wing.
It pulls a feather forcefully;
The birds begin to sing.

And with its drops of crimson
All the baby birds are fed.
The clouds roll in across the sky.
The hungering is dead.

Feed the young, they live!
Blood is meant to give.

"The Philosopher's Stone"

A sizzling pile of ash,
Pish! Pish! Pish!
An ember burns inside the mound,
Swish! Swish! Swish!

A spark goes off with a flash,
Pish! Pish! Pish!
A hundred embers all around,
Swish! Swish! Swish!

A ball of flame shoots in a dash,
Pish! Pish! Pish!
Fire crackles, flames abound,
Swish! Swish! Swish!

The motion hits the ground in crash,
Pish! Pish! Pish!
The phoenix stands upon the ground,
Swish! Swish! Swish!

Author's Afterword

What a collection of poems, eh? Hopefully you got something out of them; at least some mild enjoyment, if nothing else. I started writing these with just a few in mind, and here we are, with more than thirty completely finished (albeit of varying lengths). And in case it were not incredibly obvious, I'm a sucker for ABCB rhyme schemes. That, and rhyme schemes in general. They're like the rainbow sprinkles on the top of the literary sandwich. That was a bad analogy.

Quickly moving on, as mentioned in the introduction, this poetry collection was completed for a college course entitled "Self, Society, and Cosmos". As part of the course's instruction for this particular capstone project, each student is meant to respond to the following questions: How do you see yourself in the cosmos? Can we still find the presence of magic, religion, and science in western society? And finally, have your ideas on magic changed since the beginning of the course?

I see myself as a part of the much larger and much greater whole. The universe is filled with infinite working parts, all doing different things yet still connecting perfectly with each other. If there's no magic anywhere else, there is at least magic in that.

The second question is far more clear-cut than the first. With such specificity, my response is quite simple: modern western society views the three in order of importance with science being first, religion coming second, and magic coming third. Believe it or not, this is a very new way of thinking, only coming into the forefront of society in the last few hundred years.

The final question, which serves as the closing to this collection of related poetry, brings another relatively simple answer. Have my ideas on magic changed since the beginning of the course? No, they haven't. How far my ideas on magic stretch is up to your interpretation, of course. I will say that learning about these ancient histories, ancient peoples, and ancient ways of life was both interesting and thought provoking. I recommend doing the same if you find yourself with enough time to kill.

And with that, I close out this collection. If this were a narrative book, I would throw in some secret references to following books here. Maybe a joke that only makes sense if you know the story, or a hint at some shocking character developments. This is not, however, a narrative book; therefore it gets none of those things. If you were looking forward to them, too bad! Maybe you can send in a complaint to the author.

Rock on,
Nathan Lathroum